I0774422

Library of Congress Number: 2023905191
IBSN: 979-8-9880151-0-9

Written By Isela Arredondo
Edited by David Walters

This is dedicated to all the kids that want to learn how to use their money to have the best life possible.

What is money?

It is a form of exchange for goods and services.

Money is a tool.

What does the money tool look like?

Penny

1¢

$0.01

Nickel

5¢

$0.05

Dime

10¢
$0.10

Quarter

25¢

$0.25

What does paper money look like?

One Dollar Bill

$1.00

There are various common combinations of coins that equal a dollar:

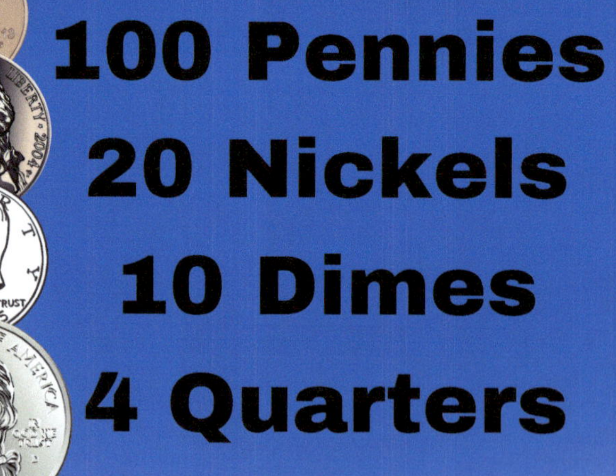

100 Pennies

20 Nickels

10 Dimes

4 Quarters

What other coin combinations can you come up with that will equal one dollar?

Five Dollar Bill

$5.00

There are various common combinations of coins that equal five dollars:

500 Pennies

100 Nickels

50 Dimes

20 Quarters

What other coin combinations can you come up with that will equal five dollars?

More Paper Money

What different combinations add up to ten dollars?

What different combinations add up to twenty dollars?

What different combinations add up to fifty dollars?

What different combinations add up to one hundred dollars?

What are other forms of money?

Checks

A paper form of money that you fill out and sign that comes out of your bank account.

Credit Cards

A thin rectangular piece of plastic or metal that allows you to borrow money that you have to pay back to the credit card company.

Digital Money

Money that can be used through an application on your computer or phone.

Can you think of places where you might use these different forms of money?

Where can you keep your money?

Piggy Bank

The money that you put in is the money that you are able take out.

Bank

When you put your money in a bank, it has many ways to grow.

And there are many other places to keep your money.

Knowing how to spend or save money can change your life.

If you had $5.00, what would you like to use it for?

Because money does not grow on trees, where does it come from?

We will discuss that in our next book.